Could this be the end of the Time Warp Trio?

The gladiator stood over us and raised his trident overhead. He jabbed down at Fred, Sam, and me helplessly tangled in the net. The trident was heading right for us when . . . when Sam thrashed around with his sword again . . . and miraculously knocked the trident aside. It stuck harmlessly into the sand.

The gladiator grunted in surprise and tried to stab us again with the trident. Fred swung his wooden sword and knocked the trident aside. The gladiator stabbed again. I knocked it aside.

"Hold still," yelled the frustrated gladiator. "Die like true gladiators."

"We'd really rather not die at all," I said.

"We use ancient fighting arts," said Sam.

"Yeah, give us your best shot, Gladiweenie," said Fred.

Fred's last crack was, as usual, just a little bit more than really needed to be said.

The gladiator grabbed the trident with two hands. Before any of us could even hope to knock it away, the trident plunged. . . .

THE TIME WARP TRIO BOOKS

See You Later, Gladiator

See You Later, Gladiator

by Jon Scieszka

illustrated by Adam McCauley

SCHOLASTIC INC.

New York Toronto London Auckland Sydney
Mexico City New Delhi Hong Kong Buenos Aires

ISBN 0-439-38994-1

12 11 10 9 8 7 6 5 4 3 2 1   2 3 4 5 6 7/0

Printed in the U.S.A.   40

First Scholastic printing, September 2002

To Eric "Wild Man" Hickey—
one of the true greats in
All-Out Big-Time Basement Wrestling.

—J. S.

For Shali, and for Eli,
two great warriors from the hui.

—A. M.

See You Later, Gladiator

I

"**Y**ou who are about to die salute me!"

"You have got to be kidding," said Sam.

The big guy who had spoken waved a net and a long-handled pitchfork in front of Fred, Sam, and me.

"He sure doesn't look like he's kidding," said Fred.

The fork-waving guy crouched in front of us. He wore a loincloth and sandals and a mean look on his face.

"I swear I put *The Book* away in a safe spot so we wouldn't get time traveled into any more trouble," I said. "Maybe he isn't a real gladiator, and maybe this isn't really Rome two thousand years ago."

"Yeah," said Sam. "And maybe I'm Santa Claus and maybe this is the North Pole."

I looked around for a way out. We stood in the

middle of a little outdoor arena about the size of a small backyard. A tall wooden wall circled all around us. Our sneakers sank into deep sand. There was no way to escape.

"Now fight," said the gladiator, getting impatient.

"I cannot believe I let myself get dragged into this time-travel-try-to-find-that-disappearing-*Book* thing again," said Sam.

"Ah, what's the big deal?" said Fred. "It's just a

little accident. This could be a great chance to see some real wrestling."

"Just a little accident?" squeaked Sam, his voice rising like it does when he gets excited. "Then why don't you explain the little accident to our friend with the trident."

"With the what?" said Fred.

"With that big fork he's getting ready to poke us with," said Sam.

"Oh yeah. I knew that," said Fred.

Sam pushed Fred forward. Fred looked up at the gladiator. He looked back at Sam. "I got it under control." Fred took off his World Wrestling hat and bowed. "Greetings, gladiator guy. We have come from far away to see some real wrestling. See I was telling Sam that even I could whip this one guy named Gladiator back in our time, but I wasn't talking about—"

The gladiator twitched like a rattlesnake.

One second Fred was hold-ing out his hat. The next second his hat was speared on the end of the trident.

"—about you . . . I wasn't

3

talking." Fred stared at his suddenly empty hand.

The gladiator flipped Fred's hat off, then pointed the trident to three swords stuck in the sand. "Now fight."

Fred backed away slowly.

"We're not really the fighting kind of—"

"*Arrrrggghhh!*" the gladiator yelled, and attacked. We all dove and grabbed a sword.

"Oh man," said Fred. "That's not fair. These are made of wood."

Sam held his sword in front of him with two hands. "I don't think our new friend really plays fair. Do some magic, Joe. Say something. Get us out of here!"

I tried to think if I knew any gladiator knockout spells. I remembered reading some kind of gladiator spell in *The Book*. But as usual, that was our problem. We had to find *The Book*.

"Excuse me, Mr. Gladiator," I said. I didn't know exactly how you should talk to an ancient Roman gladiator. But I figured it wouldn't hurt to be polite. "My friends and I dropped in by accident. And we'll be on our way just as soon as we find our *Book*."

4

The gladiator twirled his net.

"I don't think we're getting through," said Sam.

"There's three of us and only one of him," said Fred, suddenly braver now that I was the one in front of the guy's trident.

I had to think of something, quick—before the guy poked all three of us like overdone turkeys. Gladiators. Romans. The ancient Romans spoke Latin. I remembered that the gladiator spell had something to do with Latin.

The gladiator circled around us, moving in for the kill.

"Ix-nay on the ork-fay," I chanted.

The gladiator jabbed at us. We all jumped back.

"What the heck was that?" yelled Sam. "You're only making him mad."

"That's Latin," I said. "Or at least the only Latin I know. Pig Latin."

The gladiator twirled his net overhead and dropped it on us before we even knew what had hit us. He yanked a line. We fell in a heap on the sand.

"*Ahhhh!*" screamed Sam thrashing around with his sword, clonking Fred and me on the head.

"Op-stay! Eeze-fray!" I tried.

The gladiator stood over us and raised his trident overhead.

"Oh-gay away-ay?" No good.

The Time Warp Trio was about to be stuck
through with one cruel blow. And no magic trick—
Pig Latin or otherwise—could save us now.

II

But before we get poked full of holes and lose our first (and maybe last) match of *Time Warp Trio vs. the Gladiator*, I should probably explain how we got into such a fix . . . again.

I know it sounds funny, but it's all because of a book. *The Book*. A dark blue book with strange silver writing and symbols. My uncle Joe, who is a bit of a magician, gave it to me for my birthday. But he forgot to mention that this book can send its readers anywhere in time and space.

He also forgot to mention that after you go to these strange times and places, the only way to get back home is to find *The Book*.

You readers out there who have followed us before know we found all of this out the hard way.

We found you can be walked off the plank by pirates. We found you can be attacked by freaky monsters from Greek mythology. We found you

7

can be chased by your own great-grandkids. We found you can even be terrorized by characters from other books (like *Frankenstein* and *Little House on the Prairie*, to name just two very scary books).

The one thing we've never really found out is how the heck to control *The Book*. I had sworn to Fred and Sam that I would figure out how *The Book* works.

But I never really got a chance to.

We were over at my house after school, as usual. Fred was jumping around all hyper after school, as usual. So Sam and I decided to take him down.

"Freak Fred takes on all challengers for the World Monsterweight Title!" hooted Fred, bouncing up and down on my bed.

"Stone Cold Sam and Joe the Show, Tag Team Champions of the Universe, accept your puny challenge!" yelled Sam, launching himself off my chair, going for Fred's head.

"Three-Way Smackdown!" I yelled, diving at Fred's legs.

We smashed into a pileup. We brawled onto the floor. We jammed Fred into the corner by my desk.

"Atomic Butt Squash!" Sam howled, sitting on Fred's head.

Fred rolled out with both arms over his head. "DQ! DQ for disgusting move!" He staggered around, pretending to be dazed. Then he suddenly charged and tried to ram me with a two-handed pile driver. I slid him off with a judo block.

"Joe the Show knows ancient fighting arts," I said. "Use your opponent's strength against him. Ha!"

I spun and pushed Fred past me, driving him into the side of my bookshelf.

The bookshelf wobbled.

"Hiiiiii-yah!" Sam piled on.

The bookshelf teetered.

"Oooooff!" Fred squirmed around and somehow twisted on top of both of us. "One, two, three, pin!" He jumped up and raised his arms in victory. "Your new Monsterweight Champion of the World—Freak Fred!"

"Boooo," said Sam, still slumped on the floor.

Fred continued his victory lap around the room. "Freak Fred rules all wrestlers! The Hunk, Man Mountain, Killer Kowalski, the Exterminator, the Gladiator—I could pin 'em all with one hand tied behind my back!"

Fred bounced on the bed, which knocked against the desk, which bumped into the bookshelf again.

And that's exactly when a book fell off the top shelf. It dropped onto the bed and fell open to a picture of an ancient Roman gladiator, armed with a net and a trident, standing in a small, wooden-walled, sand-covered arena.

Now this would have been a very amazing and funny coincidence if the book had been any other book. But because this book happened to be a certain blue *Book* with strange silver writing and symbols on it, this was a very unfortunate and not very funny coincidence.

A familiar green time-traveling mist swirled around our Three-Way Smackdown. And before any of us even had a chance to say "Oh no," or "Here we go again," the mist had covered us up to the top of Fred's World Wrestling hat, and body slammed us back in time to ancient Ome-ray.

I I I

The gladiator stood over us and raised his trident overhead. He jabbed down at Fred, Sam, and me helplessly tangled in the net. The trident was heading right for us when . . . when Sam thrashed around with his sword again . . . and miraculously knocked the trident aside. It stuck harmlessly into the sand.

The gladiator grunted in surprise and tried to stab us again. Fred swung his wooden sword and knocked the trident aside. The gladiator stabbed again. I knocked it aside.

"Hold still," yelled the frustrated gladiator. "Die like true gladiators."

"We'd really rather not die at all," I said.

"We use ancient fighting arts," said Sam.

"Yeah, give us your best shot, Gladiweenie," said Fred.

Fred's last crack was, as usual, just a little bit more than really needed to be said.

The gladiator, completely furious now, grabbed the trident with two hands. Before any of us could even hope to knock it away, the trident plunged.

"Arrrrrr!" moaned Sam.

"I'm paralyzed!" I said.

"Everything's going dark!" said Fred.

"Brutus," called a voice. "The glory is yours. That's a win."

Brutus, our gladiator pal, kicked a not-accidental spray of sand on us and walked off.

We looked up and saw a very short bald-headed guy in a robe standing over us. He pulled the trident out of the sand between us. We sat up.

Sam patted himself all over. "We're alive."

I pulled the net off of us. "We're not paralyzed."

Fred pulled his T-shirt down. "I can see."

The bald guy looked us over and shook his head, talking to himself. "May the glorious Roman empire forgive me for sending such blockheads."

"But how come we're not dead?" said Sam.

The bald guy held the trident up to Sam's face so we could all see the blunt ends that had been buried in the sand between us and pinned nothing but our T-shirts. "Because if we use real weapons, I lose more fighters than I graduate."

"Graduate?" I said.

The bald guy smacked himself on the forehead in disbelief. "Graduate. From Ludus Gladiatorius! My gladiator school! Where I try to teach meatballs to become fighters. Look at you. How many times do I tell you—Trident fights short sword. Long shield fights long sword. Who are you supposed to be?"

Sam, Fred, and I stood up, glad to be alive, and hoping to stay that way. I figured we had the best chance to look around, find *The Book*, and get back home in one piece by pretending to fit in as gladiators.

"I'm Joe . . . um, Joe the Show that is. These are my fighting partners, Freak Fred and Stone Cold Sam. We are actually a trio . . . a Terrible Trio. We fight the Three-Way Smackdown."

The bald guy looked closely at us. He shook his head again. "Never heard of it. Must be some new thing from the provinces. You guys Picts? Gauls?"

"Americans," said Fred.

"Barbarians? Figures." The little guy rubbed his forehead. "What a headache. The emperor commands me to deliver eighty of my best fighters for the grand opening, and this is what I've got? A nice blocking move with the swords though. . . ."

"Judo," I said.

"Bless you," said the gladiator school boss. "Now listen. I need all the fighters I can get for the opening games. To graduate, it would take you three . . ." He drew figures in the sand: IV + IV + IV = VVVIII. He frowned, erased the answer, and drew more numerals: IIIVVV. He erased those and drew more: XIIIV VIIIX IXVII. He erased everything in the sand. "It would take you a very

long time to graduate. But I do you a favor. You do
me a favor."

"Sure," I said. I couldn't believe we were going
to get out of this so easy.

The gladiator boss looked around and lowered
his voice. "I let you graduate. But swear by the
gods you never tell no one you are here at Ludus
Gladiatorius. It could ruin my good name. And one
other thing—you never heard my name."

"Okay," I said.

"Okay," said Sam.

"Okay," said Fred. "But what is your name?"

"Dorkius," said the gladiator school boss.

Sam smiled, then bit his lip, trying not to laugh.

Fred laughed and tried to turn it into a cough. "Dorkius."

Dorkius scowled at the three of us. He really was a short little guy. Shorter than any of us. And his name was . . . Dorkius.

I belched out a half snort, half cough and tried to get us out of there. "Yes, sir. That's a deal. We never heard of Ludus Gladiatorius. And we never heard of . . . um . . . well . . . uh . . . Dorkius. Come on, Trio."

I ran for the wooden door out of the arena before Dorkius could change his mind. Sam and Fred followed. But if we had known then what we know now, we would have begged Dorkius to flunk us and keep us right there in Ludus Gladiatorius.

I V

We ran down the hallway next to the arena, laughing and shouting and whacking the walls with our wooden swords.

"Dorkius? Can you believe the guy's name is Dorkius?" I laughed.

Fred hacked a stone column with a quick left-right-left sword attack. "We were incredible out there. And now we're going to graduate as real gladiators."

"Right," said Sam, adjusting his glasses with one hand, trying out his sword with the other. "Very impressive. But now I would suggest we find *The Book* and get out of here before things get worse like they always do."

Fred jabbed Sam with his sword. "Ah, what are you so worried about?"

Sam blocked Fred's jab and returned one of his own. "Oh, maybe gladiators with real swords,

18

gladiators with real tridents, gladiators looking to really rip us into little pieces!!"

"Sam's got a good point," I said, interrupting his list of terrible things that might happen to us. "But where do we start looking for *The Book* in all of ancient Rome?"

"I've been thinking about that," said Sam.

"Now we're really in trouble," said Fred.

"*The Book* almost always ends up being in the most obvious place, right?" said Sam, ignoring Fred. "So where is the most obvious place for a book in a gladiator school?"

The three of us stopped and thought. I scratched my head with my sword. "A gladiator library?" I guessed.

"Exactly," said Sam. "So all we have to do is find the—"

Suddenly Fred looked up. "Wait a minute! What is that?"

Sam and I flattened against the wall. We heard the faint sound of clanking metal, voices, and growling. It seemed to be getting closer.

"A whole army of gladiators coming to fight us?"

"A whole pack of wild tigers and lions coming

to eat us and the army of gladiators?"

Fred lifted his nose and shook his head. "No, no, it's . . . *food!* Come on!"

And before we could protest or argue, Fred charged down the hall. We chased him around a corner and right into a huge room full of guys eating, drinking, laughing, and yelling.

Imagine the craziest lunch hour you've ever seen at your school cafeteria. Add about one hundred pounds of muscle on each person. Dress everyone up in loincloths, leather belts, some arm and leg armor and not much else. Then turn up the volume and the number of people smacking each other around. Then you might begin to imagine this gladiator lunch.

"Perfect," said Fred.

"What about our plans to find *The Book* in the gladiator library and green mist out of here before we get ripped into little pieces?" said Sam.

"This is perfect," said Fred. "Free food, and while we eat, we just casually-like ask where the library is."

Sam and I looked at each other. We realized that for maybe the first time in his food-loving life, though probably just by accident, Fred had a good

20

idea. We made our way through the mess of large guys chowing down. It might have sounded like our school cafeteria, but the heaping table of food was like nothing I've ever seen at school lunch. We tucked our swords in our belts and piled our plates with olives, eggs, meat, some kind of stew with little chickens in it, apples, grapes, and honey cakes.

I led us over to the calmest looking table I could find, hoping no one would notice three pretty scrawny guys in jeans, T-shirts, and sneakers crashing their meal. We sat down. Luckily the two guys already sitting there barely looked up from slurping down their food.

We hunched over our plates, doing our best to look as mean and tough as everyone else.

"Uhmmmph," said Fred with a mouthful.

"Mrrumruh?" asked Sam.

"Blawawa," I agreed.

We stuffed down handfuls of grub. We used our fingers. We didn't wipe our mouths. We dropped food everywhere, and basically broke every rule of polite dining we could. We were doing a fantastic job of looking nasty until the gladiator sitting next to Sam let loose a sudden belch.

Sam, Fred, and I all had to laugh.

21

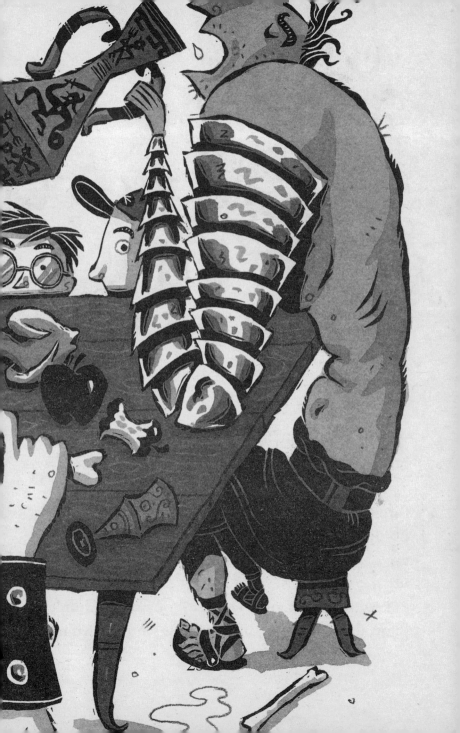

Fred leaned forward and popped out a nice "*bruuup!*" of his own.

The gladiator looked up. One eye was sliced through with a scar that went from the top of his head down to his upper lip. He fixed his one good eye on Fred, and barked a huge three-part "*buur-urrrp-churf!*"

Fred shook it off. This guy obviously didn't know that he was messing with our school belching

champion. Fred took one deep breath, paused like an ace relief pitcher at the top of his wind-up . . . then released a five-second sonic-boom "*BUUUU-UUUURRRRRRRRRRRRRRRF!*"

The burping gladiator locked his one scary eyeball on the three of us. I got the feeling that we had somehow managed to get ourselves in trouble . . . again.

25

V

The one-eyed gladiator rose slowly from the table. He stood towering over the three of us. He looked down, and you're not going to believe it, but he nodded and almost smiled.

"It is right to follow the ways of nature," he rumbled. "Be free in releasing your winds." Then he went off to load up on seconds.

Fred, Sam, and I sat frozen for a second, then cracked up.

"Freak Fred, your new Monsterweight Belch Champ," said Sam, raising Fred's arm in victory. We laughed and slapped Fred on the back.

The other gladiator at our table smiled and spoke. "A fellow believer in the body's natural functions." This other gladiator was a smallish guy, looking more like somebody who would work in an office, if they had that sort of thing in ancient

Rome. "But laugh now. Because soon we will all be part of a most unnatural circus."

"Circus?" said Sam.

"Great," said Fred. "I'm an excellent juggler."

"I don't think he means that kind of circus," said Sam.

"It has been declared a national holiday to last one hundred days. The opening of the new amphitheater built to hold fifty thousand citizens."

"You gotta be kidding," said Fred. "I think Yankee Stadium holds sixty thousand."

"The great writer Juvenal puts it best I think." The thoughtful gladiator looked up for a minute, remembering the exact words. "'The people who once made rulers, armies, and all else, now want just two things—bread and circuses.'" He swept his arm to take in the whole roomful of gladiators feasting and laughing. "Ten thousand of us—of little more importance than the ten thousand animals who will go to slaughter before us. We are that circus act."

"Well that's a pretty depressing kind of circus," said Fred. "Why don't you guys just go out there and put on a good show?"

27

"The emperor has promised that for these open-ing ceremonies, any gladiator who wins his match will be freed and granted citizenship. The crowd also can spare the life of a good fighter with their thumbs up. Thumbs down means you die."

"On second thought, I'd rather not graduate," said Sam.

"Who are all of these guys?" I asked.

"Criminals, slaves, losers in the lottery of life. Each one now is a gladiator. Each one fights in one of the gladiator styles:

"Those three hitting each other are called bestiarii. They fight the animals.

"The hairy fellow there fights with long shield and short sword.

"There is the round-shield-and-dagger man. Called a Thracian. A good omen for him per-haps—the emperor Titus favors Thracians.

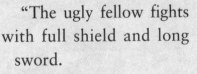

"The ugly fellow fights with full shield and long sword.

"That one over there uses the trident and the net."

"Brutus," I said.

"Yow," said Fred. "How do you know all this gladiator stuff? Are you a gladiator teacher?"

The sad-eyed gladiator gave a little bow. "I am called the Professor. I was a teacher in Carthage, a city far across the sea. I was captured and sold into slavery. My only chance for freedom is this—defeat my opponent and win my Roman citizenship."

"How do you plan to do that?" said Sam. "These guys look pretty big, not to mention mean."

"Ah, they don't look so big," said Fred. "Man, if I had a crack at these fakers I'd give 'em a left."

Fred punched left.

"I'd give 'em a right."

Fred punched right.

"I could take any one of these guys and throw him and pin him and—"

"Fred—" I tried to interrupt him.

"I'd grab him like this handful of slimy chicken bones—"

"Uh, Fred—" I tried my best to stop him.

"—and throw him right over my shoulder like—"

Fred tossed a sloppy handful of chicken crud over his shoulder to demonstrate. Unfortunately the chicken mess didn't drop harmlessly on the floor. It splattered on the very large, unbelievably hairy chest of a gladiator standing right behind Fred and listening to every word.

I pointed behind Fred.

The Professor whispered his name, "Horridus."

But it was way too late.

31

The gnarly gladiator grabbed the back of Fred's jeans with one ham-size fist and held him up like a sack of doughnuts.

The gladiators all around us laughed and roared.

I wasn't sure what Horridus planned to do next. But I didn't think he was going to show us his gladiator library card. And I knew he wasn't going to congratulate us on following the ways of nature.

VI

But before Fred, Sam, and I get any deeper into Time Warp trouble, I want to make sure you are getting the real picture here.

When I say this gladiator was "large" and "hairy," I don't mean he was as tall as your dad and had a few hairs growing out of his nose like your uncle Bob. I mean this guy was *huge*. Huge like if he wanted to sit down, he would have to use three chairs.

And hairy?

I mean *hairy* like your dog's fur on his shoulders and all down his arms right over the back of his hands. Hairy like paintbrushes coming out of both nostrils and ears. One monster eyebrow thick as a black headband. Clumps of toe hair you'd need a lawn mower to cut. That's the kind of hairy I'm talking about here.

I'm sorry you probably don't feel like eating lunch anymore, but I'm glad you get the real picture.

So this huge, hairy gladiator picked Fred up. He flipped Fred head down, pinning his arms to his sides in a giant two-handed grip. There was no way Fred could even wiggle.

"Yikes," said Sam. "He's going to slam him in a Piledriver. We've got to do something Joe."

I didn't think this was the time to try any more Pig Latin. I knew this wasn't the time to match force with force. Then the answer came to me. Judo. Redirecting force. Using your opponent's greater force against himself.

As I think about it now, I'm surprised I didn't even stop to worry that Horridus could squash me like a little bug. But that's the kind of friend Fred is. I know he would have done the same for me. I just knew I had to do whatever I could to save him from getting dropped on his head two thousand years or so before he was born.

I jumped on top of the table. I stood in my ready stance, perfectly balanced.

"One-on-one? Ha! That's nothing," I sneered, trying my best to look tough. "I challenge you *and* anyone you choose to beat me two-on-one."

"Yeah," yelled Sam, pumping his fist. Then he thought about what I had just said, and his mouth hung open and froze.

Horridus turned in surprise.

Even Fred, upside down, looked a bit shocked.

Horridus laughed. "And who are you? Crazius? Scrawnius?" He turned Fred sideways and tucked him under one arm like a loaf of bread. He palmed the top of my head with one *large* and *hairy* hand like I was one of those miniature souvenir basketballs.

For some reason, I suddenly thought of the phrase "Do or die."

35

"I'm Joe the Show," I said ducking out of his grip. "Put Fred down, and I'll beat you and any other gladiator in a test of strength."

"Oooooh," said the group of gladiators beginning to form a circle around us.

"Ohhhhh," moaned Sam, holding his head.

Horridus set Fred down. "Only two of us?" He laughed with his buddies and turned to pick a friend.

The Professor at our table pulled me to one side. "I didn't tell you," he whispered. "Horridus is the toughest of them all. He's won all his matches for five years in a row. But he returns every year because he loves to fight."

"Great," said Sam. "Out of all these mugs, we have to insult the all star of the All Stars. Say, you don't happen to have a thin blue *Book* with silver designs, do you Professor?"

"It's all about forces. Redirecting your opponent's forces," I said, more to convince myself than anybody else. And I almost had myself convinced. Then Horridus's friend stepped forward.

"Brutus," said Fred. And that's exactly who it was. Fred jumped up on the table to stand next to me. "Let's get out of here, Joe."

Brutus bowed and smiled a classic bad-guy smile. "No wooden swords now. Prepare to do battle with real weapons." He held up a real trident.

"Perfect," I said. I jumped off the table and put an empty plate on the floor. "This is your target. I will stop you two from hitting it with the trident."

Horridus and Brutus looked at me like I was crazy.

Fred and Sam looked at me like I was dead meat.

I held the trident above the plate, pointy side up. I had Horridus and Brutus grab as close to the top as possible. I crouched down near the handle a foot or so above the plate.

"Okay, tough guys. Hit the plate with the trident. Give it your best."

The two gladiators pushed down with half strength, expecting to smash the plate. I pushed the handle sideways so it bounced harmlessly off the floor.

"Yeah!" yelled Sam, seeing what I was up to. "Joe the Show!"

Horridus frowned. "We weren't really trying."

"Try again," I said.

The two beefy gladiators jammed the trident down. I knocked it sideways so it missed the plate.

The gladiators could have tried all day and never hit the plate. The secret of judo and karate is never to meet a force head on. A small force from a sideways direction can easily redirect a greater force.

"Joe the Show!" cheered Fred.

Brutus growled. "Now we really try." The two gladiators pushed down with all of their strength. I batted the handle to the side. The trident hit the floor, flew out of their hands and under the table. The plate sat there untouched.

"Joe the Show defeats Horridus and Brutus in the Two-on-One Showdown!" yelled Fred.

The circle of gladiators around us laughed and cheered. Sam and Fred each held up one of my arms in victory.

But when we turned and found ourselves face-to-face with the pointy end of the trident, our raised-arm victory pose quickly turned into something more like surrender.

"Hey, Joe won fair and square," said Sam.

The guy holding the other end of trident was, of course, Brutus. He didn't look happy. And like those bad-guy wrestlers who smack other wrestlers with folding chairs after the bell, he didn't look like he really cared about being fair and square.

VII

Brutus jabbed at us with his trident. "Now we try my test of strength. One of me will try to stick all three of you."

Fred, Sam, and I backed against the table. We held up our only protection—our wooden swords.

"Now just one minute," said Sam. "Joe won. If you want a rematch, you'll have to ask the World Gladiator Foundation."

That stopped Brutus for a second. He actually looked like he was thinking about it. Then he answered Sam's challenge the way bad guys always answer after they lose. He attacked.

Sam fell back and planted his hand right in a plateful of food. I saw his face light up with an idea like a giant cartoon lightbulb going on over his head. Sam grabbed a handful of grapes and pitched them at Brutus. The little round missiles bounced off Brutus, Horridus, and the gladiators at the next table.

Horridus picked up six bread rolls in one hand and fired them back at us.

We ducked.

The rolls bonked off the heads of six rowdy gladiators behind us. They jumped to their feet, looking for whoever had hit them.

Fred picked up on Sam's plan and smiled a huge smile. He scooped up two handfuls of leftovers. He yelled at the top of his lungs, *"Food fight!"* Then he sprayed the room with olives, figs, chewed-on drumsticks, and fish bones.

In five seconds, the whole room exploded. Food and bodies flew back and forth. It looked like a classic Three Stooges food brawl.

Fred, Sam, the Professor, and I ducked under the table to dodge the rain of garbage.

"Wow," said Fred.

"Quick thinking," said the Professor.

"Let's get out of here," I said.

"Right," said Sam, his brain already working on the next part of the plan. "Professor, where would they keep books or manuscripts here at the gladiator school?"

"I've seen scrolls that Dorkius keeps in his villa," said the Professor.

"That must be where *The Book* is," said Sam.

"Can you take us there?" I asked.

A whole chicken plopped on the floor and slid between us. Fred grabbed it and chucked it back into the fight.

The Professor looked at us. I'm sure he was trying to decide what good it would do him to look for a book with three strange kids.

"If we find our *Book*, it will help win you your freedom," I said. It just popped out of my mouth. I didn't really think about it or know how it was true. I just knew it was true.

The Professor looked me in the eye. He knew it was true. "Follow me," he said.

We stayed low and crawled through a mess of

sandals, legs, apples, pears, and stomped-on stuff, no telling what food it used to be. We safely reached the end of the tables and sprinted for the large wooden double doors.

Fred grabbed a black iron ring to swing the door open.

"*Book* and home, here we come," said Sam.

Fred looked back at the room full of yelling screaming food fighters. "See you later, gladiators." Fred pulled the door. I could already almost feel the weird twirling feeling of the green time-traveling mist taking us home until . . .

. . . the doors swung open and we ran right into Dorkius and a wall of armored bodyguards.

VIII

We bounced off the armored chests of the body-guards and fell back. Dorkius took one look at the crazy scene in front of him and yelled a command. The bodyguards smashed their shield and swords together in a noise more horrible than twenty school fire drill alarms put together.

We froze. The food-fighting gladiators froze. Dorkius stepped forward.

"Gladiators!" he yelled. "What are you—nuts? Our emperor Titus honors you with the opening of the grand arena. And you cover yourselves with garbage. To the baths, and then to Rome!"

Everyone roared. I couldn't tell if this was a happy roar or a mad roar. I didn't have a chance to ask, either, because we were quickly pushed by the beefy guys with shields through the doors at the far end of the hallway.

The doors led down a hallway to an open exercise yard. From there the whole crowd of gladiators split off into heated rooms, dropping their clothes and jumping into different pools.

Fred, Sam, and I looked at each other. The Professor took off his loincloth and sat at the edge of a long tile pool. He and the other gladiators rubbed oil on themselves and started scraping it off with curved metal blades.

"What is this?" said Fred.

"This," said Sam, "is a Roman bath."

"I don't see any bathtubs. And I don't see any soap," said Fred.

"They don't use soap," answered Sam. "You rub on the oil, then scrape dirt and oil off with that metal piece."

"No way," said Fred.

"You three, into the baths," barked one of the bodyguards. "The carts leave for Rome as soon as everyone is clean."

"Joe," said Sam. "You'd better get us out of this right now."

We put down our wooden swords. We slowly unlaced our shoes and took off our socks. No one else seemed to notice us. They were all busy getting in and out of the pools and rubbing and scraping themselves. We got out of our jeans and stood there in our underwear.

Sam gave me a very nasty look over his steamed-up glasses. "I mean it, Joe."

We heard a loud commotion at the other end of the baths.

"It's Horridus and his friends," said the Professor. "Quickly, into the caldarium. The steam will hide us."

We gratefully followed the Professor into a steam-filled room connected to the main pool

room. The four of us slid into the warm steamy pool so just our heads were above water.

"Ah," sighed the Professor. "Whatever you say about the Romans, you must congratulate them on their baths."

"How can you say that?" I asked. "Didn't they make you a slave?"

"Of course," said the Professor. "But they are still amazing engineers. Have you seen the aqueducts that carry water for miles? The bridges? The roads?"

"And check that out," said Fred, pointing into the next room. "A five-seater toilet, with running water."

"They rule the world," said the Professor. "And when I win my citizenship, all of that world will be open to me. Do you know what that means?"

I looked at the Professor's face through the shifting steam. I thought of Rome as the America of two thousand years ago. I didn't know if I could ever understand it all, but I could see how important it was to the Professor.

The baths were suddenly filled with the noise of the bodyguards bashing their shields again. "To the wagons! To the wagons! To the wagons!"

Everyone hustled out of the pools and into their clothes. We blended in with the crowd loading into the back of seven or eight big horse-drawn wagons. We sat on wooden benches in still slightly soggy underwear, nine or ten guys in each wagon. Before we knew it, we were bouncing down a rough stone road that cut straight through a warm countryside of grass and tall pointed trees.

Fred looked over the edge of the wagon. "So what's so special about the roads? They look pretty rough to me."

"This is one of the most famous Roman roads," said the Professor. "The Via Appia. The Appian Way. Built for the Roman army. Built to last hundreds, even thousands of years."

We looked back down the road. The long low buildings of the gladiator school grew smaller in the distance.

"Good-bye *Book*," said Sam between bounces. "Good-bye chances of getting home. And now I think I'm getting seasick." The cart rocked from side to side. "I don't even want to know where this is going to lead us."

"Where all roads lead to," said the Professor. "Rome."

"Ohhhh," moaned a sick-looking Sam.

"Maybe *The Book* is there," I said. "It always seems to turn up in the most difficult place to get to. Remember the Hoboken Library?"

"Don't remind me," said Fred.

The Professor looked puzzled. "What is a Hoboken? And what is this *Book* that is so powerful?"

"A book that drags me into trouble no matter how I try to stay out of it," said Sam.

"It's a very old book of things that have happened in the past and things that will happen in the future," I tried to explain without really explaining.

"Oh," said the Professor. "Like the prophecies of the Sibyl."

"Uh, right," I said. I had no idea what the prophecies of the Sibyl were, but they seemed to answer the questions of the Professor. And that was good enough for me.

"Then we must find *The Book* and all win our freedom," said the Professor.

"Wouldn't that be nice," said Sam sarcastically.

The warm sun, our huge lunch and bath, and the rocking of the cart lulled us into silently watching the country roll by. I closed one eye. The air smelled dry and freshly green. I closed both eyes. The sun flickered through the rows of trees. Sounds and smells and heat swirled. I stood before three massive gladiators. They were all armed with swords and shields and daggers and tridents.

I held up my wooden sword to protect myself.

51

My helmet slipped over my eyes. I was blind. They attacked. I spun around, jumping, twirling, and chopping with my sword like Jackie Chan. I knocked out the gladiator with the short sword. I flattened the gladiator with the full shield. I pinned the gladiator with the net and trident. The crowd cheered.

Then something large and dark hit me from behind. I was down. I looked up at the crowd. Half of them held their thumbs up. Half of them pointed their thumbs down. I couldn't tell who had more—thumbs up for citizenship and life? or thumbs down for death?

Thumbs up?

Thumbs down?

The crowd roared.

I X

The crowd roared. And I suddenly snapped awake. There really was a crowd roaring. Men, women, and children lined the road. Most wore long shirt-like things and sandals. Some threw flowers and chanted the names of their favorite gladiators.

"Horridus! Horridus!"

"Go Nefarius!"

"We want Doofus!"

It was Monday night TV wrestling brought to screaming life. The gladiators stood in the parade of wagons. They waved and flexed their muscles. The crowd cheered.

"Look," said the Professor. "Rome."

Just ahead of us rose a golden-colored city. Arched and columned buildings covered the hillsides. Crowds of people wandered everywhere. We passed through a gate in a tall stone wall.

"Check those guys out," said Fred.

A row of Roman soldiers lined both sides of the gate. They were an amazing sight in red shirts, metal chest and shoulder plates, helmets, swords, daggers, and spears. One of the soldiers with a fancy brush on the top of his helmet held up his hand to stop our carts.

"He looks just like that alien who always fights Bugs Bunny," said Fred.

"That's Marvin the Martian," said Sam. "And I think you've got it backwards. It's Marvin who looks like this guy from two thousand years ago."

The Professor looked at Sam like he was a Martian.

A blue chariot pulled by two black horses rumbled in front of us. It was quickly followed by a stream of people, most wearing something blue, running and cheering and chanting.

"On their way to more of the circus," said the Professor. He looked like he didn't approve of this part of Roman life. "Gambling away their money, their time, even their lives to fight for their team, Blue or Green or White or Red."

"Sounds like a crazy fan I know," I said, looking at Fred.

Fred whacked me with his hat.

We rolled into the city, through winding streets and surging crowds. Then we were suddenly in front of a soaring white stone stadium. Three rows of arches, one on top of the other, stood crowned by more columns and tall wooden flagpoles.

"The Colosseum," said Sam in amazement.

"It is a colossus, isn't it?" said the Professor. "It is called the Flavian Amphitheater, but I think Colosseum is a much better name."

"Folks will probably agree with you in a few thousand years," said Sam.

The stadium covered what would have been a good couple of city blocks. I saw statues in the arches, banners flying, the whole thing curving away on either side, the crowd pressing and cheering. Our carts rolled through one of the bottom arches into the cool darkness inside.

"Wow," said Fred. "That was just like being in the middle of the Yankees World Series parade."

"Yeah, just like it," said Sam, "if the Yankees got to kill the Padres after they beat them."

"What's with all the arches?" I said.

"Seventy-six vomitoria allow the stands to be emptied in ten minutes," said the Professor.

"Oh yuck," said Fred. "You mean people go and puke up all their hot dogs in ten minutes?"

"No, genius," said Sam. "Vomitorium is the Latin word for exit. Seventy-six exits get people to and from their seats in ten minutes."

"They should try that at Madison Square Garden," said Fred. "It takes forever to get out of there."

Down under the great stadium everything still seemed like a weird mixed-up dream of going to a baseball game, a wrestling match, and maybe our own execution all together.

Stadium guards hustled us out of the wagons and shoved us down a maze of hallways. All around and above us we heard the yells of a giant crowd, a lion's roar, an elephant's trumpet. I looked down a hallway and I swear I saw a monster crocodile being loaded in a cage.

"Nice warm-up act," said Sam.

Fred, Sam, the Professor, and I were all shoved into a stone holding room. A grubby looking guy in a brown tunic walked in with a round shield and a short sword. He held out a small silver coin with a picture of a man's head on one side. "The emperor decides your fates. Capita or navia?"

"Pardon me?" said Sam.

"Heads or tails," said the Professor.

"Heads," said Sam. The guy flipped. A picture of a round building with columns, kind of like the one on the back of a nickel, turned up. It was tails.

"Heads," said Fred. The guy flipped. Tails.

"Tails," I said. The guy flipped. Heads.

"Losers all," said the coin flipper. He handed the sword and shield to the Professor. "Thracian versus Three Convicts in a fight to the death."

The door slammed and locked behind him.

Fred, Sam, and I stood together with our suddenly puny looking wooden swords. We looked at the Professor and his real sword.

"So let me guess," said Sam. "You are the Thracian and we are Three Convicts with our wooden swords in a . . ."

The Professor nodded grimly.

No one had to finish the sentence.

In the awkward silence we heard the crowd, a blast of music, and then the traditional greeting given to the emperor by the first group of gladiators in the arena.

"We who are about to die salute you."

X

We looked at our wooden swords.

We looked at the Professor's real sword.

I guess I don't need to tell you things didn't look good.

"Let's break out of here," said Fred, pulling at the thick wooden door.

"Let's just hide in here," said Sam, sitting in a dark corner.

"Maybe I can remember a spell," I said. "Think of a trick." I tried to think of anything I had seen about gladiators or escaping in *The Book*. My mind went blank.

The yells of the crowd rose and fell somewhere above us.

It was no use. I couldn't concentrate. The Time Warp Trio was about to meet its end in front of 50,000 screaming people, done in by our own friend. I felt like I was trapped in a bad dream. A very bad dream. A very real dream.

Dream.

Dream.

"Dream" was the word that finally sparked my idea.

"I've got it!" I said.

A trapdoor opened above us, letting in a shocking blast of light, dusty heat, and scary crowd noise. We didn't have a second to lose.

I quickly pulled Sam, Fred, and the Professor together. I laid out my plan just as our friend in the brown tunic burst through the door.

"The emperor awaits! Get out there," said tunic guy. He poked us up the steps built into the side of the wall.

I used the Professor's sword to cut off a piece of my T-shirt.

"Do you think it will work?" said Sam.

No one got a chance to answer because we were chased up the steps and out into the center of the wildest scene I've ever seen—the view from the middle of the packed Colosseum.

Like us, you have probably seen a baseball or football stadium on TV. You might have even been to one of those stadiums in person. Now imagine standing in the middle of the stadium. Now imagine the stadium packed full of people pointing and yelling at you.

That's where we were—standing in the bloody sand of the Colosseum, blinking in the rays of the late afternoon sun, listening to fifty thousand people howling at us.

"Run 'em through!"

"Slay the criminals!"

"Attack!"

Those are just a few of the nicer things we heard the crowd yelling.

"Our only hope for your plan is the emperor," said the Professor.

"Where is he?" I asked.

"There," said the Professor.

We ran over to where he pointed, off to one side of the stadium where a group of guys sat in a kind of luxury box.

"Here goes nothing," I said under my breath. Then I found the most official looking guy. The one with the crown of leaves on his head like I had seen on the coin. I raised my hand. "Hail, emperor. We who are about to . . . uh . . . wrestle, salute you! We

bring you a special fight never seen before. Three
against one. We call it the Time Warp Trio Blind
Ninja Smackdown."

The emperor raised his hand. He didn't look all
that thrilled.

The crowd quieted a bit.

I pulled out the ripped piece of T-shirt. "The one
gladiator is armed," I yelled. "But he is also *blind-
folded!*"

I tied the blindfold over the Professor's eyes.

The crowd went nuts.

"Unbelievable!"

"Impossible!"

"Never seen it!"

Fred, Sam, and I surrounded the Professor and drew our wooden swords.

"Spin in a circle with your sword out," I half-whispered so only the Professor could hear. "Then spin the other way."

The Professor spun. Sam, then Fred, then I each let the Professor's sword hit ours and knock us back. A few of the crowd's jeers turned to laughs and cheers.

We jumped up and closed to attack again. The Professor spun blind the other way. We knocked swords and flung ourselves back. The crowd howled in amazement.

Just like in my dream, the Professor took on all three of us. We called out to him so only he could hear. He stabbed at the sound, and then we would flop back. The Professor was a natural performer. Better than the Rock, the Hulk, or anybody I've ever seen in the ring. He rolled blind somersaults and faked big sweeping sword slashes. He jumped and twisted and spun, knocking the three of us left and right.

We closed in on him for the finale. He looked trapped.

The crowd screamed.

He pulled in his shield, then dove on top of us,

knocking all three of us into a pile below him. He stood over us and ripped off his blindfold, raising it in victory.

The crowd cheered and stamped their feet like it was the third out of the seventh game of the World Series. We stayed heaped in a pile, hot and scared and smashed in the sand. But I still got goose bumps.

Looking just under Fred's armpit, I could see a lot of fans with their arms out, thumbs up. The emperor seemed to be just looking around, not making any signal.

"What's happening?" asked Sam, sandwiched on top of me. "Did he like it? Do we live?"

The Professor held his pose like a true pro, working the crowd. "He's not sure. The people like it. But there's never been such a thing. He's looking to the keepers of Vesta's shrine. They have kept the eternal flame for hundreds of years. He needs a sign from them."

For the first time I saw a group of six women dressed in white robes lined with purple. They had the best seats in the house, just down from the emperor. The six keepers of the shrine slowly extended their arms. I couldn't bear to see if their thumbs were up or down or hidden. I closed my eyes tight.

Everything seemed to slow down. The heat of the sand, the noise of the crowd, the smell of Fred's armpit swirled. Time stretched and slowed like a river of Jell-O.

From far away in the dark, I heard the crowd cheer.

Thumbs up!

"Citizens!" whooped the Professor.

"Your plan worked, Joe. We've all been freed and declared citizens!" yelled the excited Professor, pulling us to our feet.

I could hardly believe it. Big Time Wrestling had saved our skins all the way back in ancient Rome. I made a mental note to tell my mom I needed to watch TV much more often.

The four of us approached the emperor's box to receive our freedom. We stopped to bow our thanks to the white-robed keepers of Vesta. I remember thinking our triumph was almost too good to be true.

Two seconds later, I looked over my shoulder into the sand-covered arena, and saw that our triumph *was* too good to be true.

Just like in those championship matches where the good guys beat the bad guys, the bad guys were sneak attacking after the win. Except in this case, we weren't getting bonked with folding chairs or garbage cans. We were dead in the sights of two mad gladiators, one with a sword and one with a trident. And there wasn't much doubt who they were.

"Brutus!" yelled Fred.

"Horridus!" yelled Sam.

"Run for it!" yelled the Professor.

And we did.

XI

"Stand where you are, cowards," called Horridus, swinging his sword.

"Fight like real gladiators," shouted Brutus, twirling his net.

"Pick on someone your own size," cried Sam, and we took off running.

The crowd yelled in surprise and then started cheering the chase. They thought it was all part of the show. We ran away from the crazed gladiators, but there was no place to hide. We were trapped out in the open.

"Where is a good vomitorium when you need one?" said Sam, running right behind me.

And just like that, granting Sam's wish, a trapdoor opened in the sand ahead of us.

"Head for the door!" called Fred.

But lucky for Fred and us, we didn't make it there too soon. Because out of the opening there half-jumped, half-slithered the giant crocodile we had seen being loaded below. He was just as surprised to see us as we were to see him. The shocked reptile stood there blinking in the sudden sunlight. That gave us just enough time to run a wide turn around him and into the trapdoor opening. Brutus and Horridus would have to go through the croc to follow us.

Fred, Sam, the Professor, and I stumbled down stairs in the dim light. We saw the top of the crocodile's cage being lowered to the next level of the arena. That was where we came in. That would be our way out.

"Jump!" said the Professor, pointing to the top of the cage. We did.

Our sudden weight on the top of the cage must have surprised the workers letting down the cage by ropes from down below. We dropped like a rock and landed with a thud. We crawled off the top of the cage and found ourselves standing in the hallway with three very surprised workers staring at us. We took off before they had time to recover.

I remember reading this question once. "Which runs faster—fear or anger?" The fearful four of us answered that question without a doubt.

We ran down
the twists and turns
and up the steps of the
underground passageways
until we suddenly found ourselves standing outside
the Colosseum. We hid our swords. The Professor
stashed his shield in the doorway, and we tried to
lose ourselves in the crowd.

"Nice work, Professor," said Fred.

"Citizen Professor," I said.

"You'd be a killer wrestler back in our day," said
Sam. "Speaking of which—now where the heck do
we find *The Book*?"

I looked out at the streets of Rome. They seemed to head off in every direction. We drifted away from the Colosseum with the crowds of Romans coming and going.

"There are publishing shops, the Sosii, over there in the Forum," said the Professor. "Slaves copy volumina there. Perhaps your *Book* is there."

"Sosii, here we come," said Sam, looking around nervously. "Now let's get out of this neighborhood before we run into—"

"Brutus!"

"Exactly," said Sam.

"Horridus!"

"Him too," said Sam.

"Who said that?" I said.

"Their fans," said Fred, pointing behind us. We looked back and saw our two worst nightmares running down the street toward us, cheered on by their fans.

We took off down the stone streets of Rome like they were our own racetrack. I have no idea where we ran. Sometimes we followed Fred. Sometimes we followed the Professor. We followed me. We followed Sam. We just kept running with Brutus and his trident and Horridus and his sword right behind us.

It seemed like we were in one of those old black-and-white goofy cop chase movies. Except this one was all mixed up with a tour-of-ancient-Rome movie.

We ran under fancy archways. We ran past buildings crazy with columns and Latin writing and Roman numerals. We actually ran through the middle of somebody's house—right through their dinner, with flutes playing, people leaning on one elbow on couches and eating, the whole thing like you've seen in pictures. We ran along a hill where you could see an even more gigantic arena than the Colosseum, and finally sat down under the giant arches of the water-carrying aqueduct.

"I can't run another step," said Sam.

I was just about to agree when I heard two familiar voices coming down the street toward us. Brutus and Horridus were still on our trail.

"There's nowhere to hide," I said.

We heard a noisy crowd coming from the other direction.

"Oh yes there is," said the Professor. A red chariot passed in front of us. The Professor herded us into the middle of the gang of crazy Red fans following and cheering. We stayed low and danced right under the noses of the angry looking Horridus and Brutus scanning the wave of Reds that had forced them off the street.

We stayed with the cover of the crowd for a few blocks, and then ducked into a side doorway.

"In here," said Sam.

"No way," said Fred, pointing to a mosaic sign over the door. "This sign says they have a guard dog."

"I didn't know you could read Latin," said Sam.

"I can't," said Fred. "But it doesn't take a genius to translate a picture of a mad dog and CAVE CANEM into 'Beware of Dog.'"

Sam looked impressed, then puzzled. "Hey Joe. How come this sign is in Latin, but we can understand when people talk?"

"That's a very interesting Time Warp question," I said. But I didn't have time to answer because I suddenly heard two angry voices down the street that didn't need any translation.

"Oh no," I said. "Brutus and Horridus must have figured out our trick. Which way to the bookshop, Professor? Quick!"

"This way," said the Professor, pointing with his sword. He led us past a long row of serious-looking statues, through a fancy stone arch, and up to a row of low buildings. Shutters covered the windows. A small sign hung on the door. It said CLAUSA.

"Oh no," said the Professor.

"I think I can read this Latin," said Sam. "It says, 'Forget it. You will never find *The Book*. Two very mad gladiators are about to have you for lunch.'"

"No. 'Clausa' means 'closed,'" said the Professor.

"Same thing," said Sam, flopping to the ground. "That's it. I give up."

"I should have known they would be closed," said the Professor. "Everything is closed in Rome when you want to get in. Or when it's an official holiday."

"So now what?" said Fred. "These guys aren't going to give up. We'll have to fight them."

"With one real sword and three wooden swords?" said Sam. "This isn't Monday Nitro. These guys take this gladiator stuff personally. We who are about to die and all that. Forget it."

We heard the not-too-distant sound of Brutus and Horridus calling to each other. They were getting closer. This was no time for tricks. We had to hide.

I pulled on the door. Locked.

I saw a flicker of light in a circular stone building standing by itself. "Over there," I said.

"No one is allowed—" the Professor started to say, but we didn't stick around to hear the rest.

I slipped inside the building followed by Fred dragging Sam. We found ourselves standing in the middle of one large circular room. It was empty except for a huge stone bowl with a fire flickering in it.

The Professor tiptoed in behind us. He looked absolutely spooked. "No man is allowed in here." His whisper echoed around the room. "This is the very Temple of Vesta. This is the sacred fire that must never go out. It is protected by the gods and the Vestal Virgins."

"The ladies in the white and purple robes," I said.

"They love us," boomed Fred.

"Shhhh," said the Professor. "You don't understand. If we are found here, it will be worse than fighting Brutus and Horridus and twenty gladiators together. If we are found here in the Temple of Vesta, we could be—"

"Buried alive," said a voice from the shadows.

XII

The white-robed figure who had spoken stepped from the shadows into the light of the fire. We were completely surprised to see it was a girl about our age. She even looked like someone I knew. I couldn't quite remember who.

"Priestess," said the Professor. "We meant no harm. My companions are strangers and—"

"And they have come seeking only safety and their *Book*," said the girl.

Fred, Sam, and I must have looked like that cartoon where the wolf's jaw drops down to the ground and his eyes pop out of his head. She might have guessed we were looking for safety. But how could she possibly know we were looking for *The Book*?

Our mouths hung open and we stared bug-eyed at the Keeper of Vesta's flame.

"Bu-bu-but . . ." said Sam.

"Wha-wha-what . . ." said Fred.

"We-we-we . . ." I said.

A sudden angry pounding on the door echoed through the room.

"Brutus and Horridus," said Sam.

"It has been foreseen and foretold," said the Vestal keeper, without seeming to notice. "'A trio of travelers will come to reclaim / Their missing volume the first day of new games,'" she recited from memory.

"We are them," I sputtered. "I mean them are we. We are us. The trio I mean—"

"Shhh," said the girl. "We know." She pulled out a thin blue book from inside her robe and handed it to me. "Though I've never seen a scroll like this."

"*The Book!*" yelled Sam.

I had a million questions, but the green time-traveling mist was already wrapping around us.

"But what about the Professor? He needs to be

81

a free citizen. What about Brutus? How will you stop that nasty guy, Horridus?"

"This too has been foretold," said the keeper of the flame. She calmly raised her hand in farewell and smiled a mysterious smile. I really couldn't tell what it meant. I heard the doors open and the mad gladiators rush in. The last thing I saw is still burned in my mind like a painting.

Brutus with his trident raised, and Horridus with his sword drawn charged from the left. The white-robed girl and the Professor stand calmly, hands at their sides on the right. The flame of Vesta rises in the middle, streaking everyone in light and long shadows.

The green mist rolled in one last thick cloud, covering all.

I felt myself Time Warp spinning through the years and miles to home.

XIII

I've never gotten used to that stomach-twirling feeling of Time Warping, and this trip was no exception. We flipped and flopped and wormed our way through I don't know where, until we suddenly landed exactly back where and when we had been. Sam and I sat on the floor. Fred came down from mid-jump onto my bed.

The green time mist slipped away like air leaking out of a tire. Sam, Fred, and I stared at each other like we always do after time wandering, wondering if what we had just seen could possibly be real.

Fred was the first to move. He took off his World Wrestling hat and dusted the sand of the Colosseum off his pants. "Did we just—?"

Sam nodded. "Ancient Rome."

I looked down at my sword-ripped T-shirt. "Gladiators," I agreed. "But I hope we didn't mess up everything for the Professor and that girl who saved us."

"I think everything turned out just fine," said Fred.

"How would you know?" said Sam. "You look in your crystal ball?"

"Something like that," said Fred. "Check this out." He picked up the open *Book* on my bed and handed it to Sam.

There was a picture opposite the picture of the gladiator that had started this whole mess. It was a detailed painting of a round building, ringed with columns. Our girl stood on the steps smiling. A man in the toga worn only by citizens waved from the street.

"The Professor did get his citizenship," said Sam.

In the lower left corner stood two statues, frozen in angry poses. One held a sword. The other held a trident.

"And Brutus and Horridus got turned into statues," I said. "It couldn't have happened to two nicer guys."

Fred took back *The Book*. He closed it very

carefully. He pretended to look closely at something on the back.

"And look. What's this? Right here? One ugly little guy with a ripped T-shirt, and one scrawny little guy with glasses. Doofius and Stupidus!"

Fred whacked me and then Sam on the head with *The Book*.

"Three-Way Rematch!" yelled Sam, and we both charged Fred.

We smashed into a pileup. We brawled onto the floor. We jammed Fred into the corner by my desk, glad to be home.

LATIN FOR TIME TRAVELERS

Some Basic Expressions

Hello	Salve
Good-bye	Vale
Please	Sis (si vis)
Thank you for not poking me with your sword.	Gratias tibi ago quia me gladio tuo non fodisti.

Questions

Who?	Quis?
What?	Quid?
Where to?	Quo?
Have you seen a blue *Book*?	Vidistine *Libellum* caeruleum?
Which way to the vomitorium?	Qua via itur ad vomitorium?

Signs

Stop	Sistite
Closed	Clausus, Clausa, Clausum
Beware of dog	Cave canem
Beware of large hairy men with weapons	Cave magnos homines pilosos qui arma portant

Making Friends

I'm Joe.	Joe sum.
Is that your trident?	Estne tuus iste tridens?
Look behind you.	Respice retro.
Run for your life!	Curre pro vita tua!

TURN THE PAGE FOR A SPECIAL PREVIEW
OF THE NEXT TIME WARP TRIO NOVEL:

Sam Samurai

ONE

Sam stood frozen in his ready karate pose. He spoke in a low voice.

> "Do not move an inch.
> If we're where I think we are,
> We are dead meat."

"What are you talking about?" said Fred loudly. "So we're probably in Japan. I'll bet we can get some great noodles and sushi."

I wasn't sure exactly where Sam thought we were,

but I knew we weren't in Sam's house anymore. Fred, Sam, and I were standing on a low wooden platform that covered most of a small dirt floor room. A flickering fire burned in a rectangular pit cut into the side of the platform near the dirt floor. A metal teapot hung over the fire from a long hook in the ceiling. In the jumpy light I could just make out a few mats around the fire pit. There were no chairs, no tables, no beds.

I whispered to Sam and Fred as I looked around the room, "It sure looks like Japan, but I think we are okay because there aren't any samur—*aaiiiieeee!*"

A crazy, wild scream exploded out of me. All three of us jumped against the wall, because there in the farthest, darkest corner of the room, looking just like the guy in the picture Sam had shown us, sat a samurai warrior in full battle gear.

Layers of shiny black and red strips of armor covered his shoulders. A breastplate and skirt kind of thing of the same strips tied with gold cords covered his chest and lower body. He wore black leather and chain arm covers, padded shin guards and foot covers, and a wild gold-horned black hel-

met sprouting side flaps. A thin gold sliver shaped like a new moon topped everything off.

He sat motionless in the corner, staring at us like we were rats in a trap.

"Oh . . . my . . . ga-ga-gosh," gasped Sam. "I told you this is what would happen."

Even Fred, who is pretty hard to rattle, sucked in a nervous breath.

I quickly bowed my most serious bow like I had seen in Sam's samurai movies. "Gee Mr. Samurai guy, we are very sorry for time warping into your house like this. All we have to do is find our *Book* and then we'll be on our way. Okay?"

The samurai stared back at us, motionless.

"Fine? Is good? *Hola? Si?*"

The samurai stared back at us, motionless.

"Oh great," I said. "I think something's wrong with the Auto-Translator. He's not getting a word I say. Sam, you know some Japanese words. Get up here and use them."

"No way," said Sam, edging behind Fred. "I said I learned a few words. I didn't say I learned how to beg a fully armed samurai warrior not to slice off our heads with his razor-sharp sword."

Fred pushed Sam forward. "Well just say whatever you've got—hello, sorry, see ya. I don't think we want to mess with this guy."

Light glinted off the samurai's red-lipped black metal faceplate. Sam inched forward.

"Um . . . well . . . *konichiwa*, samurai. My friends and I—Joe-san, Fred-san, Sam-san—are so sorry . . . um, so *zannen* . . . for coming into your house."

A stick fell in the fire and shot up a blaze of light. The samurai seemed to look down at Sam's feet and frown. Sam looked down at his sneakers.

"Oh no." He turned to us. "Quick, take your

shoes off and throw them over there on the dirt part of the room."

"What?" said Fred. "He doesn't like the smell of our sneakers? This guy is starting to sound like my mom."

"No," said Sam. "It's terribly impolite to ever wear your shoes in anyone's home in Japan. He could cut our heads off for such an insult."

"He's definitely starting to sound like my mom," I said.

But it didn't seem worth it to lose our head over shoes, so we slipped them off and tossed them over onto the dirt floor. Sam bowed. Fred and I bowed along with him.

"Sooo sorry. So sorry," said Sam. "We are sorry, very sorry, I can't tell you how sorry, so please-don't-do-anything-with-your-sword-there-because-we-were-wearing-shoes-inside-your-house-and-we-are-stupid-heads sorry."

"Hey, speak for yourself," said Fred.

The fire blazed up again. The samurai in the shadows seemed to look down again.

"Oh right," said Sam. "We're supposed to kneel down in front of him because he is a samurai." Sam knelt down. Fred and I copied him.

The samurai stared at us and said nothing. Seconds drifted by. No one said anything. We looked at him. He looked at us. Seconds turned into minutes. No one said anything.

"I think he's testing us," Sam half whispered out of one side of his mouth.

"Well, I think I've had about enough testing," said Fred. "Tell him it's been real, it's been nice, but we've got a *Book* to catch."

"Patience," whispered Sam. "Samurai are impressed by patience and control."

"Maybe we can patiently back out of here," I said. "My knees are killing me."

"Please don't use that k-word," whispered Sam.

"Hey, check it out," said Fred. He nodded toward the wall closest to us. Three long spear poles with machete-style blades at the ends leaned against the wall.

"Those are closer to us than they are to him," said Fred. "There are three of us and only one of him."

Sam turned completely ghost white. "No, no, no. Don't you remember *Blade of Lightning*? Samurai are fast enough to take on ten guys with spears *and* swords."

It was too late. I could tell Fred had already made up his mind. He got up slowly, pretending to stretch his legs.

"Oh, that's it. Just needed to stretch the old—"

Then it all happened in a second. Fred jumped for the machete-spear weapon. His shadow flashed across the samurai.

"Look out Fred!" yelled Sam. "He's going for his sword!"

I dove for the samurai's feet and smacked my head on his shin guards. The samurai fell toward Fred. Fred grabbed the spear. He spun around to face the samurai, and as he turned he swung the spear with him. The samurai lunged. The blade of the spear caught the samurai just under the chin and sliced his head right off his shoulders.

The armored body part crashed to the floor. The helmeted head rolled and rolled and came to rest next to the fire pit. The red-lipped black faceplate stared at us in the light of the dying fire.

Sam and I stood up. Fred looked at the blade of the spear.

"Sorry?"

Jon "Mad Dog" Scieszka has wrestled into print *The Stinky Cheese Man*, *Squids Will Be Squids*, nine Time Warp Trio novels, and a lot of other books you could look up if you really want to know. He lives in Brooklyn, New York, with his wife and two children, and is the current holder of the Killerweight Home Championship Belt.

Adam McCauley's illustrations have appeared in magazines and books, and on CDs and all sorts of other wacky stuff. His first children's book, *My Friend Chicken*, was published recently. When he's not drawing, Adam enjoys playing his drums, cooking, and surfing.